Published in the United States by Grolier Books, a
division of Grolier Enterprises, Inc.

Printed in Norhaven Book, Denmark
First print, november 2006

ISBN: 0-7172-6490-2

WALT DISNEY
PICTURES PRESENTS

THE *Tigger* MOVIE

GROLIER
BOOKS

It was a tiggerific autumn day in the Hundred-Acre Wood.

"Hoo-Hoo-HOO!" Tigger happily called, bouncing through the freshly fallen leaves. "It's wunnerful to be the one an' only me!"

In fact, Tigger felt so wonderful that he decided to share his bounciness with his good friend Winnie the Pooh.

   "Howdy do, Pooh!" Tigger greeted him. "Ya
wanna go bouncin' with me?"

   "Well, I *would*," Pooh answered, "except that I
must count my honey pots for winter."

   "*Yecch!*" Tigger replied, accidentally stepping
into one. "I'll never unnerstand why you Poohs
like this icky stuff! Well, anyway, T-T-F-N,
Ta-Ta-For-Now!"

So Tigger bounced
over to Piglet's house.
"Hiya, Piglet Ol'
Pal!" Tigger called.
"What say you an' I do
a little bouncin'!"
But Piglet was
too busy collecting
firewood for the winter.

Tigger saw Kanga next. But Kanga also
had too much work to do to go bouncing.
What Tigger didn't realise was that Roo
would have loved to go bouncing with him.
But by the time Roo came running out of
the house, Tigger had gone.

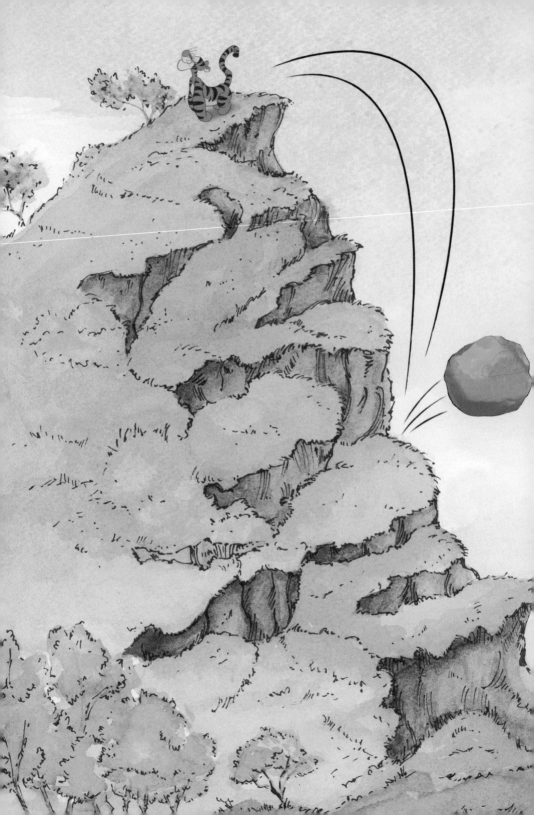

Tigger sat down on a large rock. "Why would anyone *not* wanna bounce?!" he wondered.

Tigger was sure *someone* would want to bounce with him. So he bounced off the rock and back into the forest. He didn't notice the rock had come loose! It rolled down the hill and landed—*CRASH!*—right on top of Eeyore's house!

Eeyore was okay, but his house wasn't.
It was stuck under the rock. It wasn't long
before everyone but Tigger came round
to help. Tigger still didn't know what had
happened.

Rabbit came up with a plan to move
the rock. Everyone helped him construct a
funny-looking device. No one really knew
how it worked, but Rabbit was sure it
would.

They pushed and pulled. But the rock
didn't budge.

"Hello, you blokes!" called Tigger, springing into the group. "Anyone up for a little bouncin'?"

"We have no time for such nonsense," Rabbit cried. "There's work to do!"

"What? Moving that old thing?" Tigger asked, examining the rock. "Not a problem! All you need is a little bouncing!"

"You think *bouncing* will move this boulder?" said Rabbit. "Ha ha! It's almost amusing!"

"Here, I'll show ya!" Tigger answered. He
wound himself like a giant spring and—
BOING!—unleashed his biggest bounce ever.
The rock went flying!

Unfortunately, so did Eeyore and all his friends.
Around and around they tumbled and stumbled
until finally—*SPLAT!*—they landed in the mud.

"Now that *that's* out of the way," Tigger said to his muddy buddies, "who's up fer a little fun-type bouncin'?"

"Just look at this mess!" Rabbit shouted angrily. "Everything's ruined and all you can think about is *bouncing?*"

"Well . . . yeah," Tigger innocently answered, "that's what tiggers do best."

"But we're not tiggers,"
Pooh reminded him gently.
"Ya mean, no one
wants to bounce with
me?" Tigger asked sadly.
He walked off into
the forest all alone.

"Who needs 'em anyway!"
Tigger exclaimed. "I'll just
bounce by myself . . . with
nobody else."

"But Tigger," Roo protested,
joining him, "aren't there
other tiggers? I have a mama.
Don't you have a family
somewhere, too?"

A family? Tigger had never thought of such a thing
before. It was a thrilling idea!

"A family full of tiggers, ya say!?" he asked
excitedly, bouncing up and down.

But Tigger didn't know where to find his family. So he and Roo went to ask Owl.

While Owl rambled on about family trees, Tigger accidentally knocked some pictures off the wall. Roo tried to help his friend by coughing loudly to distract Owl while Tigger tried to put the pictures back in place.

Then suddenly, while looking at the wall, Tigger had an idea! He would search for his own family tree—a tree that would be gigantical, stripedy, and full of . . . *tiggers!*

And so, with Roo's help, Tigger searched the Hundred-Acre Wood for a tree filled with tiggers.

He searched high.

He searched low.

He searched near.

He searched far.

"Yoo-hoo!" Tigger called. "Famil-eeee! Halloo?"

For hour after weary hour, the two looked, but found nothing.

The other residents of the Hundred-Acre Wood were busy, too. They were still helping one another prepare for winter.

But when Pooh, Piglet and Eeyore found out that Tigger was looking for his family, they decided to help him instead. So off they went on their own quest for tiggers.

Meanwhile, Tigger and Roo had almost given up. The tired twosome trudged back to Tigger's house.

"Where *aren't* those tiggers, anyway?" Tigger said with a sigh. "We've looked every which an' where—not to mention right over there—and not a single stripedy tree in sight."

"And just think," Tigger continued, "if there were other tiggers, we could all bounce the Whoop-de-Dooper Loop-de-Looper Alley-Ooper Bounce."

"Could you teach it to me?" begged Roo. "I'm a real good bouncer! *Please?*"

"That's ridickerous!" Tigger answered. "No offence, Roo Boy, but I think you're a little on the smallish side of tiny for that."

Roo tried the
bounce anyway,
but crashed.
Things fell all
around him.

Tigger noticed a heart-
shaped locket and picked
it up. He eagerly looked
inside the locket to see
if there was a family
picture.

But the locket was
empty. "Completely
tiggerless," sighed Tigger.
"How am I supposed to
find my family now?"

Then Tigger had a great idea. He would send his family a letter and invite them to his house.

Roo eagerly helped his pal. When they had finished, they sent off Tigger's letter. Then they sat down to wait for a reply.

Meanwhile, Pooh, Piglet and Eeyore weren't having much luck looking for Tigger's family.

Eeyore found some bouncy animals. But they weren't the right sort of tiggers.

Pooh found some stripedy animals in a tree.
They reminded him of honeybees.

It turned out they *were* honeybees—
angry honeybees!

All the while, Tigger and Roo waited
for an answer to Tigger's letter. Soon the
first snow of winter began to fall.

Roo became worried about his downhearted pal, so one night he talked to his mother, Kanga. The next morning, Kanga and Roo gathered the gang together to write a pretend letter from Tigger's family.

"'Dear Tigger,'" Owl began writing. "Now what else shall it say?"

"How about . . . dress warmly?"
Kanga suggested.

"Yes," Pooh agreed. "And eat well."

"Stay safe and sound," advised Piglet.

"Keep smiling," Eeyore added.

"We're always there for you!" Roo said.

"Wishing you all the best," Owl concluded.
"Signed, your family."

That night, they secretly placed the letter
in Tigger's mailbox.

"Hoo-Hoo-HOO!" Tigger gleefully shouted the next day. "Look what I've got! A letter from my very own family!"

Everyone smiled. Tigger was happy. Their plan was working.

"And the bestest part of all is that they're comin' ta see me—tomorrow!" Tigger added.

Everyone stopped smiling. They never wrote *that!*

"Um, where exactly does it say that?" asked Owl.

"With tiggers, ya have to read between the lines," Tigger explained.

Tigger was so excited that his friends didn't have the heart to tell him the truth. Luckily, Roo came up with another plan. They would all dress up like tiggers and pretend to be Tigger's family.

The next day, the pretend tiggers knocked on his door.

"Surprise!" they shouted when Tigger opened the door.

Tigger couldn't believe his eyes. "C'mon in!" he eagerly invited. "There's lotsa catchin' uppin' we gotta do!"

"Hey, who's up fer some family-type fun-n-games?"
Tigger offered. "I know! Let's do what tiggers do
best—bouncin'!"

"Let's do the Whoop-de-Dooper Loop-de-Looper
Alley-Ooper Bounce," cried Roo.

But when Roo tried the bounce, not only did he
crash again, but his mask also fell off.

Tigger saw that his family of tiggers were really his Hundred-Acre Wood friends. His feelings were hurt.

"We only wanted to help," explained Pooh.

"That's all right," replied Tigger, sniffling. "Somewhere out there is my family. An' I'm gonna find 'em. So T-T-F-E, Ta-Ta-For-*Ever*."

Tigger left the house and entered the cold forest all alone.

The next morning, a terrible blizzard hit the
Hundred-Acre Wood. Without Tigger, winter
seemed much colder and much more unfriendly.

"Pooh!" pleaded Roo, entering the bear's house.
"We've got to find Tigger! It's dangerous out there!"

So Pooh gently suggested that he, Piglet, Eeyore,
Rabbit and Roo form an *expotition* to find their
missing friend.

Meanwhile, Tigger tramped through the deep snow, still searching for his family tree.

Suddenly he saw the biggest, tallest, grandest tree ever!

"I found it!" he shouted, bouncing up the branches. "*Halloo!* Is anybody home?" He bounced from branch to branch, looking for tiggers.

But he didn't find a single one.

At the same time, Roo, Pooh, Piglet, Rabbit and Eeyore bravely fought the freezing weather as they searched for Tigger.

"Tigger! Tigger!" they called through the howling wind. "Where are you?"

But Tigger didn't hear them. He sat on a
lone branch and moaned. The big tree was
empty. There was no family of tiggers.

"Maybe they forgot I was coming," he said.

Just then Tigger spotted something far
below him.

It was his friends. "Hey!" he cried as soon as he had bounced down from the tree. "What're you guys doin' here?"

Suddenly there came a loud, low rumbling sound. It was an avalanche! Snow roared down the mountainside!

"C'mon, hurry up!" Tigger shouted, bouncing his friends up the tree to safety. "No time fer dawdlin'!"

Just when it seemed
that everyone was safe,
Tigger was swept away in
the swirling snow!

"I'll save you, Tigger!"
Roo cried.

There was only one
way to save Tigger. Roo
wound himself up and
unleashed the mightiest
Whoop-de-Dooper Loop-
de-Looper Alley-Ooper
Bounce ever! He grabbed
Tigger and pulled him
to safety!

"Hoo-Hoo-HOO! Ya did it, Roo!" Tigger cheered. "Ya bounced just as good as any tigger could!"

Later, when everyone was safely home, Tigger held a party for his pals.

"Ahem and ahoom!" he proclaimed. "On this most occasional occasion—my firstest ever family reunitin'— I'd like to present each of ya a present."

Tigger gave Eeyore a new house; Pooh some honey; Piglet firewood; and for Rabbit, he promised always to watch where he was bouncing.

Last but not least, Tigger gave Roo the heart-shaped locket. And inside the locket, Tigger put a picture of his very own family—his *real* family. The family Tigger had discovered he had all along.